Mountain
Rescue

Mountain
Rescue

Mountain Girl Series:
Book 3

Rose Creasy McMills

REDEMPTION
PRESS

© 2015 by Rose Creasy McMills. All rights reserved.

Published by Redemption Press, PO Box 427, Enumclaw, WA 98022.

This is a work of fiction. Names, characters, places, and incidents either are the product of the author's imagination or are used fictitiously. Any resemblance to actual persons, living or dead, events or locales is entirely coincidental.

© 2015 Cover Illustration by Shirley M. Levesque.

© 2015 Web design by Jonathan McMills: www.mountaingirlbook.com.

ISBN 13: 978-1-63232-988-2 (Print)
             978-1-63232-989-9 (ePub)
             978-1-63232-990-5 (Mobi)
Library of Congress Catalog Card Number: 2014957498

To Billy Mullens

Contents

Prologue

ELIZABETH SHIFTED HER backpack and looked up Tyler's Mountain. The trees went up and up. The mountain blocked out much of the sky and cast a long shadow, turning the valley to dusk in the middle of the day.

Wild turkeys nested in the tops of the trees and occasionally spooked and flew up with a beating of wings and frantic gobbling, startling her. A stray turkey buzzard circled about.

Elizabeth was wearing tall hiking boots with thick socks, insurance against snakes, and carrying a walking stick from the collection Grandpa had made. Thinking of Grandpa made her eyes prickle. She missed him still.

She was eighteen and had spent last night at the West Virginia farm of her girlhood. But she didn't want to be here, for the first time ever. She had a mission, though—Uncle John had disappeared, and she might be the only one who could find him.

He had said to her once, just before she'd left the farm and moved to Fairmont, that she had his gift—that she could sense things. "You've got it too. You jus' don't know it. You cain't use what you don't know you have."

It may have been the longest sentence that Uncle John ever spoke to her.

Elizabeth knew that back in the forest were many creatures—raccoons and possums, but also wolves, coyotes and black bears. Copperhead snakes hid under the edge of rocks. Poison ivy and poison oak would make your skin erupt if you touched it.

But back in the woods, too, was incredible beauty—a fairyland of tall pines, maples, oaks, ash, and beech with their canopy of green one hundred feet overhead . . . virgin timber.

The forest floor was covered with spongy moss, flowers, ferns, and dried pine needles that rivaled the lushest designer carpet. Birds seldom seen by human eyes flitted from branch to branch and trilled their piercing whistle. Deer bounded through the woods, freezing at a sound like they'd turned to stone.

The mountain was lovely and dangerous at once.

She knew he was up there hiding. She had to find him.

Chapter 1

Billy

As ELIZABETH CLIMBED the mountain late in the day, she heard scuttling through the leaves down the hill from her and stood still, listening. A squirrel? A deer? A black bear?

She hoped it wasn't a bear because there was no eluding them. They were small, agile, and could climb trees, so escaping *up* wasn't an option. She pulled her slingshot out of its holster, picked up a rock, and waited. She looked to Velvet for a response, but there was no reaction from the beagle, who was sniffing invisible rabbit tracks.

Now she heard the movement again . . . a little closer and to the right. She secreted herself behind some bushes, pulling Velvet with her. Better to face it head on than to run.

Velvet's getting old, she thought; *her senses must be dulled.*

The rustling got louder, and Elizabeth saw some movement at the edge of the clearing. Then suddenly Velvet's tail began to wag, thumping against Elizabeth's hip, and Billy stepped into the clearing.

"Billy!" Elizabeth exclaimed, then in the next breath, "You followed me!"

"I know where he might be," Billy said hastily as if he had the power to beam Uncle John home immediately. He stooped to pet Velvet who was whining and wiggling all over in an ecstatic greeting.

"Does Pearly know you're here?"

"She does and Aunt Lorena too." Lorena, Uncle John's sister, was up from Charleston to take care of Pearly and the newborn baby. Elizabeth figured they must be worried sick about her Uncle John. Why else would they have let Billy go after her?

She turned and picked up the handheld sickle she had brought along and started hacking her way through the brush angrily. "You have to go back," she said. "It's too dangerous up here."

"I want to come." Billy followed her, walking in her path, grabbing the fallen brush, and tossing it out of the way.

"Well, I don't want you to. I'll travel better alone—you'll slow me down. I don't need to be takin' care of you." She turned to face him. At that moment she realized his eyes were almost level with hers.

"I'm going with you," he said.

"No, you're not!" Elizabeth stepped forward angrily and shoved his shoulder. He stumbled backwards, blond hair flopping. "Go home!" she said, jutting out her chin.

"You can't make me," Billy said.

They stood a foot away from each other, breathing hard.

And Elizabeth realized she couldn't. Billy was a big ten-year-old. His father had been a miner and Billy had spent the last five years working the farm alongside John, his stepfather. He was no longer a little boy.

"I care about him too," Billy said quietly. "He's the only father I've got."

"Okay . . ." Elizabeth said, reluctantly. "Okay, but I'm the leader of this expedition, agreed?"

Billy stuck out his hand and Elizabeth took it half-heartedly. "Agreed," he said seriously. "Let me spell you with that," he said, gently taking the sickle out of her hand.

At lunch, they settled on a blanket of moss, their backs against a giant oak for safety. They had beef jerky, slightly stale biscuits, and apples.

"So where *do* you think he's gone?" Elizabeth asked, drinking from Grandpa's old canteen.

"There's an abandoned mine on the west side of the mountain near a hickory grove," Billy said. "One year us two hiked up there lookin' to shoot a wild turkey for Thanksgiving."

Elizabeth was silent a moment, considering.

"I remember talk of a cabin near that mine," she said. "I thought he might have gone there."

"Oh . . . the haunted cabin?" Billy bit off a piece of jerky.

"Yeah, they tell stories about it—that it appears and disappears."

"You figure they're true?"

"More than likely people just forgot where it was. It's easy to lose your way up here."

"That reminds me . . ." Billy stuck his hand in his pocket. "I brought a compass."

Elizabeth smiled at him in spite of herself.

Back at the farm, it was dusk. The chickens had climbed up the little ramp into the chicken house to roost for the night, making soft clucking sounds.

Aunt Lorena walked through the upper meadow, trailing her hands through the tall grasses—the Queen Anne's Lace, blue-flowered chicory, all the late flowers of summer.

The lovely day had faded into evening. The lightning bugs were floating in the air, and a cool breeze stirred her hair. A red sun dropped behind the mountains leaving the sky streaked pink and blue.

Billy

But she didn't notice the beauty around her. She felt restless and worried. She'd gone out to look up Tyler's Mountain in the hopes of seeing something, *anything*—a campfire, maybe. She hoped they would be alright. She hoped Elizabeth and Billy would find John and bring him back. She knew the odds were slim, but Elizabeth had worked wonders before. She was not especially surprised that her brother left. Twenty-nine years of his brooding presence, his fits and crises had conditioned her to accept almost anything he did.

And yet . . . the last five years since he had married Pearly had been so good. It seemed John had become a stable, content family man. All the things she had wished for him as a girl—a normal life—had come true.

But now this—running off and abandoning his wife, infant daughter, Billy, and the family farm. Why did he go? She'd never understood why John did what he did. All the old shame and anger she had felt as a girl came back to her.

But also sorrow—for John, whom she loved dearly and wanted the very best for.

It just didn't make sense.

Chapter 2

Uncle John

H E KNEW THEY were following him, of course, but he knew they couldn't find him if he didn't want them to.

And he didn't want them to.

The baby had been alive when he left the farm, and Pearly had been dead. That knowledge plunged him into a dark place where there was no escape. His own private hell. Even Elizabeth couldn't have reached him now.

All he could think to do was run and keep running. Try to forget . . . forget how he'd come back from his withdrawal, silence and loneliness into the security of Elizabeth devotion, the warmth of Pearly's smile, the acceptance by the community.

Now with her death, he'd slipped back to the edge of madness.

He'd dressed automatically for his escape—good boots and warm clothing—brought a snakebite kit, his rifle, matches, and a knife for skinning animals. Up here in the wilderness that was Tyler's Mountain there were streams for drinking and berries and plants he knew were edible. There was wild game, and he was a skilled hunter.

Shooting the gun and building a fire, though, could be a problem—that would give him away. His only hope was that as he went farther into the forest, they would get discouraged and turn back. He knew Billy was with her now and he hadn't counted on that. He'd known Elizabeth would come after him.

It was hot and humid from all the vegetation and he was perspiring; the sweat ran down his forehead to soak the bandana handkerchief tied around his forehead.

Have to keep moving. His thoughts were a tangle, his mind a fog. Only one thought was uppermost. Escape! It was like when he was a boy and visitors came to call. He would slip out, frantic to get away and scoot under the low back porch and beneath the house, lying on his belly on the cool dirt until they had gone, not responding to calls. Alone, hidden, safe. Safe from the inevitable difficulties of life—the ups and downs, the expectations, the pain and heartache. Protected from all the messy encounters with people.

His last night on the farm haunted him as he climbed.

He never could handle a woman in labor, and Pearly's cries from the bedroom worked him into a frenzy. She sounded like she was dying a slow, painful death. He fled the house, walking the farm's meadows in agitation.

When he came back, it was evening, and all was silent. He crept around the outside of the house and raising his head slowly, peered through the bedroom window. Tiny cries were coming from the handmade cradle in the corner, but his attention was drawn to the bed. And there was Pearly—stretched out, not moving, not breathing, hands folded across her stomach in final repose.

And he had fled.

He'd rushed blindly into the kitchen, tears blurring his eyes. He pulled food from the pantry, stuffing it into his pack, spilling oatmeal all over the floor in his haste and crunching through it on the way out.

Bursting out onto the back porch, he tripped over the cat and almost fell. As he steadied himself, he was aware of someone in the shadows.

Billy.

"Where are you going, Pa?"

John looked at the boy wearily. He had grown considerably in the years since he and Pearly had moved in with John. You could almost see the man he was going to be.

"I gotta go, Billy."

"Go where?"

"Away. Back in the mountains."

Billy's voice shook. "But why?"

"Your ma . . ." John choked on the words.

"What's wrong with Ma? The baby got borned, right?"

John pushed past him. He fumbled with the gate's latch and let himself out of the yard, leaving the gate swinging. Without a word, he started across the meadow toward Tyler's Mountain.

"Pa! Don't go!" Billy pleaded, sounding like a child.

John turned back in desperation. Better Billy be hurt and forget him sooner. "I'm not your pa."

"Yes you are!" Billy was sobbing now. "Please, don't leave me!"

John faced the mountain and broke into a trot.

"Pa . . ." Billy said brokenly.

He turned and dashed into the house, slamming the screen door, strode through the living room and dining room, up the step into the upper room, around the potbelly stove and into his parents' bedroom.

Pearly lay in bed exhausted, her skin pale, hair spread across the pillow. Billy moved to the side of the bed.

"Ma . . .?" then more urgently, "Ma!"

She stirred and took a deep breath, rolling toward him with a smile. "There's my big boy." She took his hands in hers and pulled him down for a kiss on the cheek.

"Are you alright?" Billy asked shakily.

"I'm fine, Billy Boy, just tired."

The bedroom door opened, and Aunt Lorena came in and picked up the fussing baby from the cradle. "She wants her mama," Lorena crooned at the little bundle. She gently placed the baby in Pearly's arms.

"Hello there, little Emily Elizabeth," Pearly cooed, kissing the soft head of dark hair.

Billy reached out and stroked a silky arm and put his finger into her tiny hand. She surprised him by grabbing on tightly.

"That's your big brother," Aunt Lorena informed her, sitting on the side of the bed and straightening the covers.

"Where's John?" Pearly said. "Has he seen her yet?"

"I was looking for him," Lorena answered.

There was a pause.

"He's gone," Billy said woodenly.

Lorena and Pearly looked at him.

"What do you mean?" Pearly asked.

"He's gone up the mountain. I don't think he's coming back."

Chapter 3

Poison Ivy

THE NEXT DAY Billy started scratching.

"Lemme see," Elizabeth said, reaching for his arm.

"Maybe it's fleas from Velvet," he said, turning an accusing eye on the dog. Velvet's ears drooped, and she crawled under a bush.

"Don't think so," Elizabeth said, pulling back his sleeve to reveal little blisters. "I think you've got poison ivy."

"Oh man!" Billy exclaimed.

"Try not to scratch; that'll make it spread."

"But I can't stand it!"

Elizabeth was digging around in her backpack.

"Aha! Here it is!" She pulled out a bottle of witch hazel.

"Mom puts that on cuts—it stings."

"It may sting where you scratched, but it dries it up." She took a rag and stroked the liquid on his arms and hands while Billy gritted his teeth. "Anywhere else?"

"Not yet."

They resumed their hike, heading toward where the disappearing cabin was said to be.

"Do you think *he* might get poison ivy?" Billy asked.

Elizabeth laughed.

"Not likely . . . he knows all the plants."

"Why do you think God created things like poison ivy?"

Elizabeth stopped and turned to look at him. Sometimes Billy seemed almost a man and other times a little boy. She wasn't sure which one had asked the question. "That's a pretty heavy question."

Billy waited.

"Uhhhhh, because there's evil in the world so we can appreciate the good?"

Billy considered this. He was feeling better. "I guess he also created witch hazel," he said slyly.

Elizabeth smiled.

That night they built a campfire and sat staring into it, dead tired.

"Tell me about their wedding—Mom and John's," Billy said.

"You were there. You were the ring bearer."

"I know but I was only five and don't hardly remember."

Elizabeth winced at his English but began the story . . .

The wedding of Uncle John and Pearly Blue had been the occasion of the year when Elizabeth was thirteen. It was spring and Pearly wore a cream-colored dress with little seed pearls sewed into the bodice. No one begrudged her the white dress, even though white was usually reserved for first-time brides.

John was dressed in a new dark suit and looked so handsome with his curly black hair and blue eyes that the young women in the congregation were all aflutter.

"He coulda been mine," they whispered to each other.

With her hair down her back, Pearly looked like a young girl, despite having a five-year-old and being a widow. Billy followed the couple down the aisle of Alderson Church carefully carrying a pillow with his mom's ring safety-pinned to the top. Men generally didn't wear rings in the mountains because work made them dangerous. You could get a ring caught in a piece of machinery on the farm or in a mine and tear your finger off, like had happened to Ethan Johnson.

It was a gorgeous day in late May, and the lilacs, rhododendrons, and forsythia were blooming, perfuming the air.

Reverend John Brown performed the ceremony. It seemed he had always been old, his hair a shock of white, his gray beard reaching almost to his belt, his black suit shiny from years of wear. He had watched this congregation grow up, get baptized, get married and die, but this couple was special to him.

He had married Zack and Pearly eight years ago and sat with her all one night after Zack was killed in the mine explosion. He knew the McCrearys well because he was Rose McCreary's brother and over the years, had listened to her concerns about John—his sensitivity, tantrums, problems with school, with others, his moody withdrawals. He knew, too, John's special gift for memorization, his talent for art and music. His uncanny instincts.

He had worried, along with Rose, that there would be no partner for John but they had both been wrong because here Pearly was! God had provided, and he and the community were overjoyed. *If only Rose had lived to see it,* he often thought. He could feel her looking down from heaven, though, and he told the congregation as much.

There were no other children for years for the couple—a fact the ladies of the community lamented. Then last year, Pearly became pregnant, and there was "praise the Lord" on everyone's lips.

Pearly and John had told Grandpa they were expecting a baby girl as he lay on his deathbed with the whole family present.

"How do you know it's gonna be a girl?" Grandpa's eyes, bright with fever, peered out under his bushy white eyebrows and met Uncle John's. No one could predict the sex of a child, although a lot of the older women surely tried.

"I *know*, Pa," John said.

"We're going to name her Emily Elizabeth," Pearly said eagerly, a soft hand going to her belly.

Elizabeth gasped in surprised pleasure.

There was a moment of silence.

"Hand me that there Bible," said Grandpa, propping himself up on one bony elbow. He seemed clear-headed and himself again, none of the dementia that had plagued him these last years. This brought tears to Aunt Lorena and Mama's eyes; Daddy cleared his throat.

With a shaky hand Grandpa fumbled with the pencil hanging from the string attached to the Bible and licking one finger, turned back the crinkly pages until he found the front charts where Elizabeth's Grandma Rose had recorded the family history: all the births and deaths, weddings and funerals.

Everyone in the room held their breath as he carefully scrawled in the name Emily Elizabeth McCreary under *Grandchildren*. "Now it's done, even though she ain't been borned yet," he said, sinking back on the pillows and closing his eyes. "Now I kin go . . ."

". . . and see Rose again," he added.

Chapter 4

Thunderstorm

IT WAS USUALLY dark under the tree canopy and today especially so because the sun had gone behind a looming thunderhead. The birds had stopped singing, and there was an unnatural hush. Then the wind picked up, turning the leaves upside down so their silver undersides showed. The humidity increased, and there was a rumble of thunder in the distance. Elizabeth and Billy looked desperately for cover. Elizabeth was trying for a big pine with low-hanging branches or a partially hollowed-out tree.

"Over here," Billy shouted above the sound of the rising wind.

She climbed through the dense underbrush toward the sound of his voice. It was getting darker by the minute. She caught her toe on a root, went down on one knee, and then scrambled up and went on.

Billy had found an overhang, an outcropping of rock, and scooted back underneath with Velvet in the soft dirt and dried leaves. Gratefully, Elizabeth crawled toward him as the storm began in earnest—thunder and lightning and pouring rain. The three of them huddled under the ledge, almost a small cave, and were cozy and dry.

This looks like one of those rains that goes on for days, Elizabeth thought sleepily. She hoped not. She wondered where John was and if he'd found shelter. She wondered when she'd begun to think of him as "John" instead of "Uncle John."

John had sensed the storm coming long before the young people and had pushed on until he reached the mountain cabin. He remembered very well where it was located and could have found it with his eyes closed. He didn't believe the cabin was haunted or that it appeared and disappeared. "Tall tales," he muttered to himself. He realized he was starting to talk to himself again—something he hadn't done for years. But he didn't care about anything anymore.

The cabin was as he remembered it—simply furnished with a few wooden chairs, a table and two single beds with closely woven hemp mattresses. He started going through the few drawer in the side of the table and found candles and matches. Hurriedly, he set one up and lit it as the storm hit, and it got black as night.

He lay down onto the bed with a sigh, using his jacket as a blanket, and prepared to wait it out. They wouldn't be hunting him now—not in the rain. He was safe for the moment. As he watched the flickering candle, a scene from his past rose up before him—a waking nightmare . . .

It was fall and school had started up. Every morning after chores and breakfast, John rode behind his sister Luella on Dolly, their mule, three miles to the one-room school over at Beaver Creek. Mules were stubborn and when Dolly decided to stop for a bit, there was no moving her. Often they were late to school because of this but many children were late, having to do work at home first and often coming from long distances. No one had cars, although occasionally they would see one fly by, leaving a trail of dust, scaring livestock. The last one the family had seen was the dinner topic for a full week.

On this day John and Luella had wanted to take a shortcut through the woods but when they tried to turn Dolly off the usual path, she had balked and stopped walking altogether. She just stood there with both ears back and her tail switching to flick off the flies.

The children stayed on her back. John, who was behind, lay backwards over her brown rump and looked up into the trees.

"It would be faster to walk than to ride this stupid mule," Luella said.

"It's a long walk, though," John said. "I wish Pa would let us take a horse."

"Pa doesn't want to deal with Dolly," Luella said, "and he knows you can work with her."

Out of the blue, Dolly uncocked her hoof and began walking toward the school. John righted himself and grabbed onto his sister's waist.

That day was when the trouble started.

"Now class, for next Monday I'd like you to memorize the first stanza of Edgar Allan Poe's poem *The Raven*." Miss Carpenter, who was called an old maid because she never married, turned from erasing the blackboard. "A stanza is the first section," she added. She was wearing a dark gray dress that hit her mid-calf and matched her iron gray hair pulled back in a bun.

"Would someone like to read it aloud now?" She scanned the classroom, her eyes softening as they fell on John, hunkered down at his desk. He was one of her favorites . . . so smart. "John?"

John cringed then got up reluctantly and walked to the front of the room:

"Are you alright?" Billy asked shakily.

"I'm fine, Billy Boy, just tired."

The bedroom door opened, and Aunt Lorena came in and picked up the fussing baby from the cradle. "She wants her mama," Lorena crooned at the little bundle. She gently placed the baby in Pearly's arms.

"Hello there, little Emily Elizabeth," Pearly cooed, kissing the soft head of dark hair.

Billy reached out and stroked a silky arm and put his finger into her tiny hand. She surprised him by grabbing on tightly.

"That's your big brother," Aunt Lorena informed her, sitting on the side of the bed and straightening the covers.

"Where's John?" Pearly said. "Has he seen her yet?"

"I was looking for him," Lorena answered.

There was a pause.

"He's gone," Billy said woodenly.

Lorena and Pearly looked at him.

"What do you mean?" Pearly asked.

"He's gone up the mountain. I don't think he's coming back."

Once upon a midnight dreary, while I pondered weak and weary,
Over many a quaint and curious volume of forgotten lore . . .

"Wait, where's your book?" Miss Carpenter asked.

"I . . . I . . ." Dagnabit! He should have brought his book and pretended to read!

"How much of it do you remember?" the teacher said in awe.

John hung his head.

"Recite some more, John," she said kindly. "See how far you can get."

While I nodded, nearly napping, suddenly there came a tapping,
As of some one gently rapping, rapping at my chamber door.
"'Tis some visitor," I muttered, "tapping at my chamber door—
Only this, and nothing more."

When he had finished reciting the poem—all eighteen stanzas—there was silence in the room, punctuated by the snapping of the fire in the stove.

"Why . . ." Miss Carpenter had her mouth open in amazement. "You only just read that poem this morning?"

John nodded.

"I've heard of this," the teacher addressed the class. "It's called a photographic memory. I guess John won't have to memorize for Monday," she said lightly.

The class tittered at her little joke, but the big boys in the back were silent.

"Kin I sit down?" John asked. He found being the center of attention excruciating.

"Of course, John."

He hastened to his seat. Luella in the back of the class with the big girls caught his eye and smiled. Maybe it would be alright but he didn't think so.

Chapter 5

Bullying

RELEASED OUTSIDE AT recess, John gloried in the fresh air, sunshine, and the beauty of the hazy, blue mountains. He moved away from the knots of children into the trees and sat on a mossy log. Listening to the birdsong, he was totally content.

Then he heard branches snapping in the woods behind him. A deer? He turned slowly so as not to frighten it and saw the three big boys who sat in the back of the classroom making their way through the underbrush.

His first instinct was to run, but they quickly encircled him.

"So, *teacher's pet,* what you doin' out here all by your lonesome?" Bubba Johnson sneered.

"How's about you say that *luverly* poem for us again," another added.

The third boy snickered, moved close behind John, and breathed hot puffs on the back of his neck.

"I think he needs to be taught not to show off, don't you Harry?" Bubba said softly, stooping to pick up a stick.

Suddenly, Luella appeared through a stand of pines. "You leave him be," she said in a strident voice.

"Well lookee here. He's got his big sis comin' to protect him." The three shouted with laughter.

"You touch him and I'll go straight to the principal," Luella said firmly.

There was a moment of silence—a standoff. The two other boys looked at Bubba. "Shucks, he's not worth the trouble. C'mon boys," he said. But as Bubba turned to leave, he shoved John hard into a thorn bush. His cronies grinned.

Luella ran to help him up as the boys moved off.

John had scratches all over his arms and face but worse than that, he was shaking and had "gone into hisself," as the family called it.

"Johnny, are you okay? They've gone now." Luella tried to get him to meet her eyes.

He shook off her hand and began pacing, distractedly counting his steps aloud. Luella didn't try to stop him. She knew he used this as a calming technique—an attempt at reordering his world.

The bell rang in the distance, signaling an end to recess.

"We gotta go in," she said urgently.

John didn't hear her. His eyes glassy, he turned at the edge of the clearing and resumed his march in the opposite direction.

Luella knew she couldn't leave him. She sat on the log and prayed for the spell to pass, eyes closed and hands clasped so tightly the knuckles were white. "Please Jesus," she repeated over and over.

Then she heard more crashing in the woods. Were they coming back? Luella picked up the stick Bubba had dropped and turned to face the intruders.

Principal Owen Masters emerged. "The bell rang, you two. Let's go!"

I can't tell him about the bullying, Luella thought. *They'll beat John up another day.* "John was feeling poorly, Mr. Masters. I've been sitting with him."

"Nonsense," Mr. Masters said, taking John's arm, "recess is over."

"No! Don't!" Luella began but the damage was already done. John was like a captured cat—swinging and clawing, kicking and biting, tears streaming down his face.

The principal was unprepared and caught a couple of blows before he held the panicked boy at arm's length, then yanked him forward, grabbing him around the waist from behind and lifting him off the ground.

John flailed helplessly in the air, sobbing.

Luella watched in despair, having seen this before and knowing the only solution to John's spells was to leave him alone until he got over it.

Suddenly, John went into convulsions, stiffening up and quaking all over. Mr. Masters laid him carefully on the ground. "What's the matter with him?"

"It's a fit," Luella said. She took her handkerchief out of her pocket, folded it, and put it between John's teeth so he wouldn't bite his tongue. *This is the end,* she thought. *They'll never let him come back to school this time.* She watched her little brother sadly as the tremors began to pass, smoothing the hair from his forehead.

John woke with a start. It was night in the cabin and still raining hard. The candle has burned out and it was pitch black.

Why had he been born so different? Why had life always been so hard? Pearly had given him security and love and the courage to rejoin the world, to live a normal life. And now she was gone. The weather matched the anguish in his soul as the rain pounded on the roof and wind howled around the cabin.

He rolled on his side and stared into the dark until he fell asleep.

Chapter 6

Danger

ELIZABETH AWOKE IN the morning to the sound of a whippoorwill's distinctive call from a tree outside the cave. *Whippoorwill . . . whippoorwill.* Its persistent song reminded her of the rooster's crow that would wake her in the morning when she was a girl on the farm. Just try to sleep with that racket going on. The rain had stopped and the sun was glinting through the trees. The intermittent drip of rain off the leaves made a pleasant sound. *Whippoorwill . . .*

Elizabeth rolled over and shined her flashlight at Billy's bedroll, which turned out to be empty. She felt annoyed and a little worried. Where had that kid gone? This was exactly why she hadn't wanted him to come along, she said to herself. She didn't need someone to look after.

She pulled on her boots and laced them but then paused when she smelled meat cooking! She ducked her head and crawled out of the cave, stopping astonished on her hands and knees at the sight of Billy cooking over a smoking campfire. Velvet was sitting at his feet, eyes shining in ecstasy. "Bacon! You brought bacon!" she exclaimed.

Billy started. "Well, it's been smoked so it won't spoil," he said defensively.

"It smells wonderful!"

Elizabeth got to her feet and came over to study his technique. Billy had sharpened the end of two thin sticks and threaded the bacon on them, reminding Elizabeth of the ribbon candy they had at Christmas. He was holding the sticks over the fire and turning them carefully. The grease was dripping down and sizzling in the fire. "Did you have that in your knapsack?" she asked quietly.

"Yeah." Billy glanced quickly at her.

"Well, it was raining so hard last night that we didn't have to worry about animals," she said. "Tonight, though, we'll have to hang a bag of food from a tree."

Billy nodded. "Breakfast?" he said, holding out one of the sticks.

"Yum," Elizabeth said, getting out the biscuits she had brought along, slicing them in two and inserting the bacon. "Delicious!" she said enthusiastically after the first bite.

They ate their fill, fed Velvet some, and still had leftovers. Billy put the rest of the cooked bacon in his backpack.

"We should probably throw it out," Elizabeth said.

"But what about lunch," Billy wheedled.

So the bacon came along.

"Which way today?" Billy asked as they started diagonally up the side of the mountain.

"I know there's a stream over this way," Elizabeth answered. "I thought we might follow it for a while."

"You talk different now," Billy said, falling in behind her.

"What do you mean?"

"In the past, you woulda said, 'There's a stream over *yonder.*'"

Elizabeth considered. Since they'd moved to Fairmont five years ago, she was aware that she had lost some of her accent and stopped using many country expressions.

"I guess you're right. Does it make me sound uppity?"

Billy grinned. "Naw, it's alright."

Soon they heard the sound of rushing water. Swelled by the rain, the little stream was impressive, tumbling over rocks and cascading down the mountain. There was no place to cross so they followed it uphill. As they got higher, the terrain was rougher and water cut between large rock masses. Still there was a bank of pebbles and they stuck to it, though it shifted under their feet somewhat.

Then as they rounded one huge rock, there was a black bear standing in the stream slapping at a fish in a small pool. The bear didn't see them and Elizabeth grabbed Billy's arm and froze. "Don't move," she said in a tense whisper.

Billy gasped.

"Don't run, and don't climb a tree," Elizabeth said quietly.

At that moment the bear noticed them. He rose up on his back legs and sniffed in their direction then opened his mouth and gave a warning growl.

"The bacon," Elizabeth said in horror as he dropped to all fours and started toward them through the stream. "Throw the knapsack," she said urgently.

"But our food," Billy said.

Her nails dug into his arm. "Do it!"

As the bear picked up speed, sloshing through the water, Billy yanked the bag off his shoulder and with all of his strength, threw it to the opposite bank.

The bear immediately changed direction, and as he clambered up the bank, Elizabeth and Billy backed carefully into the woods behind them. When they were out of sight, they turned and ran.

The bear was busy going through Billy's knapsack.

Danger

Once a safe distance away, they sat panting while their heartbeats slowed. "That was a close call," Elizabeth gasped out.

"All my stuff," Billy lamented.

"We're alive—that's what counts."

Chapter 7

Critters

AFTER THE CONFINEMENT of the stormy night, John was hungry. Someone had left cans of beans and corn and an old box of Corn Flakes in the cabin. He ate some of the corn and decided he needed to forage for meat and fresh greens. First of all, he needed wood for the fireplace. The cabin was going to be the base of operations for now.

He walked to the edge of the mountain and looked out. Clouds drifted lazily below him, the air was crisp and fresh, and the mountains stood majestic in the morning mist. The rain was still dripping from a thousand trees and the leaves of the ground plants all held sparkling drops in their upturned leaves.

Tears stung John's eyes—tears at the beauty, tears of pain.

He searched for greens first, filling his sack with the leaves of dandelions from a small meadow near the cabin. Afterwards he set a trap for a rabbit for dinner and then went in search of honey.

He remembered a bee tree from the last time he'd hiked up here with Billy. When he located it, he was relieved to see it was still active. He cut a branch from a bush, leaving the leaves attached. He would need to smoke the bees out to get at the honey.

John hesitated a moment, match in hand. Would Elizabeth see the smoke? Perhaps she'd turned back in the rain. He knew she hadn't, but he had to eat. If they got close, he'd move on. There were a number of these small, abandoned cabins up here, built by old mountain men—trappers and hunters, moonshiners escaping the law. He'd find another.

He lit the branch and when it began to smoke, he stuck it in the hole in the tree. Bees buzzed angrily, then vacated, swarming in the air in confusion. John reached in easily and pulled out a chunk of comb dripping with golden honey.

At midday, Elizabeth and Billy came upon a small level clearing, a delight after all the mountain hiking. It was covered with lush meadow grass and wildflowers and was obviously an area where deer grazed and bedded down.

Billy threw himself on his back, bending down the tall grasses. "Oh man, this is swell!" He rolled from side to side. "Let's stay here forever!"

Elizabeth turned her face up to the sun, stretching out her arms, spinning round and round. She felt like a kid again.

Billy propped himself up on his elbows and watched her with a grin.

"I see buttercups," she exclaimed, wading through the grass. She stooped and picked a bouquet, putting a yellow flower behind one ear.

"I'm hungry," Billy said.

"You know, sometimes there are berries around a clearing like this," she said. "Let's check the edges by the woods."

They cut through to the other side of the field, leaving a path behind them of bent-down grass.

"Raspberries!" Elizabeth shouted.

Since losing Billy's knapsack to the bear, they had been relying on her small store of beef jerky and stale cornbread. Fresh fruit would taste wonderful.

"Watch out for thorns," Elizabeth warned as Billy began to pick berries into his hat. But careful as they were, they still ended up with scratched hands from where the bushes had protected their fruit.

But the reward! Berries so sweet and fresh that they melted into juice and trickled out the sides of their mouths. Elizabeth looked at her stained hands in mild dismay. "Now we'll have to find a stream to wash up." But neither of them moved, just sat in the grass full and satisfied.

Aaauuwwwwooooo . . .

Suddenly they heard Velvet's bay. She had been off hunting rabbits and they had forgotten about her in their feeding frenzy. Now she was tracking them down.

"Here girl," Elizabeth called and the grasses parted and the little beagle appeared, tail wagging in doggie joy. She jumped in Billy's lap, bowling him over and licking the raspberry juice from his face. "You may not need the creek after all," Elizabeth laughed.

Then Velvet settled in her lap but as Elizabeth stroked the smooth coat, she felt a lump, then another. "What's this?" She ruffled back the dog's fur to expose a tick clamped onto the skin with its mouth pinchers and drinking its fill of the dog's blood. Then she found more. "Omigosh, she's covered with them! Billy help me out."

They picked off the tiny black parasites, and Billy smashed them between two rocks. It was the best way to kill them because of their hard bodies. Velvet stood obediently, panting in pleasure at all the attention.

"Grab them with your fingernails close to the skin and yank," Elizabeth instructed; "otherwise you'll lose the head."

"I know. I've seen ticks before," Billy muttered. *She treats me like a kid, he thought.* "It's the grass," he added. "They love to hide in grass."

"I know. I didn't think about it. Uh oh . . . check yourself," she said, hand going to her hair.

And sure enough, ticks were lunching on them too—on their scalps, hiding under their shirts, inside the waists of their pants, on the back of their legs.

"Yuck!" Bill exclaimed, jumping up.

"I'll do you, and you do me," Elizabeth said. She felt creepy all over.

They busied themselves removing ticks from themselves and each other ("like a couple of monkeys," Billy said) and killing them with the rocks. By the time they were done and had made their way back to the stream for a wash up, the sun was behind the mountains, and they needed to set up camp for the night.

Chapter 8

Smoke

THAT EVENING ELIZABETH had brought
down a quail with her slingshot, so supper was a
treat. Billy had made a spit out of three green branches,
two of them forked in a Y shape with the other end
stuck in the ground on either side of the fire. The third
branch pierced through the carcass suspended over the
flames. He and Elizabeth took turns rotating the meat
so it cooked evenly on all sides. The smell made their
mouths water. Velvet lay between them, watching the
cooking meat with rapt attention.

"Smells like chicken," Billy said appreciatively

"Yummy," Elizabeth said.

"How much longer do you think?"

She squeezed the small thigh. "Done!"

They lost no time cutting it in two and each taking half, adding the raspberries they'd picked that day to the meal.

"All we need is some potatoes and we'd have a feast fit for a king," Elizabeth said.

Velvet sidled up close to Elizabeth, whom she knew to be a soft touch, eyes pleading, tongue lolling out.

Elizabeth laughed. "You are *such* a beggar," she said, rumpling the dog's ears. She pulled off a drumstick and handed it over.

"How'd you get so good with the slingshot?" Billy asked, his mouth full of grilled meat.

"I've been practicing," Elizabeth said wiping away some juice that was running down her chin. She stared into the fire, remembering the first time she'd ever seen a slingshot.

"What are you doing?" Elizabeth sat down on the edge of the back porch beside Uncle John. He froze in the middle of carving what looked to be an animal.

People didn't speak to Uncle John in those days, but Elizabeth had had enough of that. She was eight years old, and her draw to Uncle John was so strong that she couldn't stop herself, although she'd probably get a scolding.

Uncle John looked around to see if anyone was watching. "Whittlin'." He resumed the quick, energetic strokes against the wood with his pocket knife.

Elizabeth watched, moving a bit closer. Uncle John inched over against the post. "A horse, right?" she said.

"Right." The corner of his mouth twitched. He shaped some ears pointed eagerly forward, a mane falling over one tiny eye.

"That's beautiful," Elizabeth sighed.

Uncle John paused. His eyes slid sideways to take in his niece. "You shouldn't be talkin' to me. You'll get in a heap of trouble."

"Show me how you do that," Elizabeth persisted.

Uncle John hesitated, then suddenly . . . "Let's make you a slingshot!" He jumped up and went to the dogwood bush, cutting off a forked branch. "This'n will do." He sat back down beside her. "You got your knife?"

Elizabeth pulled out her little pocket knife and for about an hour the two worked, their heads bent together as they removed the bark from the Y, smoothed the ends, and worked the wood until it was smooth with no splinters.

Grandpa walked by silently at one point. Mama peeked from behind the curtains. But no one stopped them.

"There ye be!" John exclaimed. "Get your daddy to fit some rubber straps and a leather pouch on there." Then he stopped and stood up, putting away his own knife. "Jest one thing."

"What?" The little face turned up to him trustingly.

"Don't kill any animals except for food."

"I won't," Elizabeth promised.

Grandma appeared on the porch. "Lizzie, you come set the table now, ya hear?"

As it grew dark, they occasionally saw eyes glinting in the woods around them, attracted by the smell of cooking meat.

"You think they'll attack?" Billy said uneasily.

"Naw . . . those are just 'coons and possums and such," Elizabeth said, cleaning up from their feast and sniffing the air, ". . . and a skunk somewhere."

"I'll be right back," Billy rose, wiping his hands on his pants. "C'mon girl," he whistled to Velvet. There were no outhouses up here. That was for sure.

The eyes watched as he went a bit away from the campfire for privacy. As he was turning to go back, he saw smoke way over on the next ridge. "Liz! There's smoke!"

She hurried into the dusky woods.

"You think it's him?" he asked.

"It's got to be. That's about where the cabin ought to be and no one else is up here, surely." She stood watching the smoke curl peacefully above the trees. "Remember where you saw it. We'll head there first thing in the morning."

Smoke

Velvet saw the smoke, too, and sensed Elizabeth and Billy's excitement. She had always known where John was—she caught his scent easily now. She didn't understand this game all her people were playing—members separating and going off in different directions. The pack was meant to be together.

She sniffed longingly in John's direction and whimpered softly. Then when Elizabeth and Billy turned back to the campfire to bed down for the night, she turned up the mountain, homing in on the ridge where she knew John was, and took off at a steady trot.

Chapter 9

The Disappearing Cabin

JOHN STOOD IN front of the cabin watching their campfire flicker through the woods. It looked to be five miles away but distances were hard to estimate out here—getting somewhere always took longer than you thought it was going to.

If I can see them, they can see me, he thought. He'd need to move on tomorrow.

He looked at the little cabin with a touch of sadness. It had been nice to have its shelter. Maybe he shouldn't have cooked but he just couldn't eat the rabbit raw. *Well, what's done is done. They won't come tonight.*

In the morning, he packed up and closed the cabin, leaving it clean for the next person passing through—the code of the mountains.

He'd been hiking only about an hour when he heard rustling down below him. It couldn't be Billy and Elizabeth—they couldn't have made it to the cabin that soon. He considered the other possibilities, reaching over his shoulder and fetching an axe out of his knapsack. Whatever it was, it was making a beeline through the underbrush straight toward him. He readied himself and waited.

Then Velvet burst into the clearing, nose to the ground, tail going.

"Velvet!" John squatted down, and the little beagle jumped into his arms, covering his face with ecstatic licks. "How are you, girl?" He patted and stroked all over the wriggling brown and white body and gave both ears a good scratch.

When the pup had quieted, he sat on the ground and thought, stroking her head. He hadn't counted on their having the dog with them. Hounds could track anything anywhere. If Velvet was here, Elizabeth and Billy couldn't be far behind. And the dog would lead them right to him.

He considered. He could try to chase Velvet off (fat chance), or he could let her tag along. He dug into his knapsack for the remains of last night's supper and gave the dog a good chunk of rabbit meat. She wolfed it down greedily.

"C'mon girl," he said rising to his feet and starting up the hill. The dog followed obediently. It might be good to have the hound along—for hunting, for company. He felt the deep emptiness in his soul.

"Where has Velvet got to?" Elizabeth wondered aloud as they trekked through a stand of pines, their fallen needles soft underfoot.

"Huntin' probably."

"It's not like her to be gone so long, though."

"Maybe she went home."

"Could be . . ." Elizabeth allowed, but it made her uneasy. Surely they would have heard the dog barking if she were in trouble. "Now where did we see that smoke?"

"Up aways but I think we're close. Wait, there's the cabin!" he exclaimed as it rose up out of the mist.

But another ten minutes of walking produced nothing. It was a foggy day—the tops of the mountains shrouded in mystery. Clouds floated by or hugged the hills. They continued walking through the wet foliage, only able to see a few feet ahead.

"Are you sure we're going in the right direction?" Elizabeth asked as she came up by Billy.

"Yeah—it should be right over there." He studied his compass and pointed into a bank of fog.

"Okay. Let's go then."

After a few minutes, Billy said excitedly, "There! I see the chimney!"

But more walking yielded nothing. The two stopped in frustration.

"I think we're going in circles," Elizabeth said. "This darn fog!"

Billy took out his handkerchief and wiped the back of his neck. They were both decidedly damp. "Well *I* think it's the disappearing cabin thing."

"Don't be ridiculous!"

"Seriously! One minute it's there, and the next it's not."

"Billy, it's a foggy day, and you can't see much of anything."

"Well, according to my compass, we should have been walking in the front door several times already."

They looked at each other, breathing heavily from the climb. Suddenly, a blue jay screamed behind them, and they both jumped and whirled around. And there was the cabin.

"Gosh dang!" Billy said nervously.

Elizabeth stepped purposely toward the front door. "He's been here alright," she said. "There's wood been chopped."

"Someone or *something's* been here," Billy said ominously.

Elizabeth went inside to look around. It was very neat and looked untouched but the ashes were warm and Uncle John's aura floated in the air like dust motes. She squatted to pick up a small, round object on the floor. It was a horehound drop.

She smiled. Uncle John and his candy. She emerged triumphantly from the cabin and presented Billy with the sweet.

"I'll be," Billy marveled.

"We're hot on his heels."

"So we move on?" Billy looked at the cabin.

Elizabeth followed his gaze wistfully. It would have been nice to spend the night under a roof with a fireplace. "I reckon we better," she said.

"Good, cuz I'm not staying in there."

Elizabeth considered him. The mountain people sometimes believed in ghosts and strange happenings deep in the dark, impenetrable woods. The terrain had a mysterious, foreboding feeling about it and gave rise to stories—stories that some believed. "Let's go," she said.

Chapter 10

The Mine

JOHN CLIMBED STEADILY with Velvet at his heels; the dog was happy to be along. As long as the pup was with him, Elizabeth couldn't use her to track him, he figured. She couldn't trail him with the dog, true, but John knew if Elizabeth used her powers of intuition, she could sense him and find him. He felt her coming up the mountain now, a couple of hours behind him. They'd probably been to the cabin by now.

He was deep in thought when he felt the ground collapse under his feet and he was falling, landing hard on his left ankle. He just had time to wrap his arms around his head for protection before he hit the ground.

He lay for a minute not moving and then put his arms down slowly. Was he hurt? Bruised and scraped for sure. He sat up carefully and looked around and up.

The roof of an abandoned mine had collapsed under his weight and he was now in a tunnel with the ground some distance above his head. He could see trees and the sky through a jagged hole; dirt and small rocks tumbled in intermittently. Inside it was dark, the walls held in place with wooden scaffolding, an old track for carts carrying coal disappeared down the shaft.

John tried getting to his feet and then grimaced in pain as his left ankle throbbed. Was it broken? He couldn't tell but the pain was intense. He sat down heavily on a beam from the ceiling. *Praise the Lord that I'm alive,* he thought. He realized with surprise that he wanted to live after all.

Then he heard Velvet whimpering. The dog crawled on her belly to the edge of the hole and peered down at him.

John looked up at the little beagle. "Go get Elizabeth, girl," he said. The pup whined louder but didn't move. "Guess that kind of thing only happens in the movies," he muttered.

He closed his eyes and began to breathe deeply, searching for his niece, trying to connect. He knew he was in trouble. There was no way he could get out, hurt as he was. He could die up here. His only hope was Elizabeth and Billy, and now he *wanted* them to find him. He put all of his inner strength into contacting Elizabeth, hoping she'd be receptive, open herself to it.

The Mine

Elizabeth was sleeping on a bed of moss under an oak tree. She and Billy had hiked all morning, eaten from what they had left and were resting before the afternoon's climb. She woke with a start.

Billy was lying on his stomach, watching ants carry leaves back and forth. "I thought you'd never wake up," he said, sitting up.

Elizabeth yawned, still tired. She got to her feet brushing off her pants.

"Which way?" Billy stood, too, and took up the walking stick Elizabeth had brought along.

"Ummmm . . . this way, I guess," Elizabeth said foggily, indicating a break in the trees to her right. Billy dutifully trudged ahead. She followed more slowly and soon he was a distance ahead. After a while, he turned and came back to her. "What's the matter? You okay?"

Elizabeth did feel a little dizzy. She sat down on a stump. "I don't know—something's wrong." The middle of her forehead felt hot and she reached up to touch it.

"You got a fever?" Billy asked.

Suddenly, Elizabeth leaned over and threw up in the weeds.

"Land o' Goshen!" Billy exclaimed, jumping back.

"Something . . ." she said, closing her eyes. Then they snapped open. "It's Uncle John. He's hurt! We're going the wrong way!"

Billy was speechless, his mouth open.

She leaped up and started back the way they had come, almost running. "C'mon!" she called over her shoulder.

John was getting thirsty and hungry and had lost track of time. How long had he been down here? The sun had moved for sure—he must have passed out briefly. He tried moving his leg, and it hurt even more than it had earlier. He groaned.

A dog snout appeared over the ragged edge of the hole.

"Hey, puppy." John looked up at her. Loyal dog.

Perhaps this will be the end of me, John thought. He felt no fear, only a great sadness. *Let it be over then.* He settled himself down to wait, getting as comfortable as he could. Then he heard Velvet barking and recognized their voices greeting the dog. He knew he was saved and tears of gratitude stung his eyes. "Praise God," he muttered thickly.

Chapter 11

Reunited

ELIZABETH WAS IN the mine with Uncle John now. She had tied the rope to a tree and lowered herself down. The three of them were trying to devise a plan to get him out, an endeavor complicated greatly by his injury. Billy had gone into the woods to gather some firewood. It was mid-afternoon and the shadows were already deepening. Elizabeth and John sat across from each other.

"Why'd you run?" Elizabeth said accusingly. "How could you leave your baby girl?"

"Why'd you have to come after me?" John said heatedly. "Why couldn't you jest let me be?"

"The baby needs you, and Billy, and Pearly."

"Pearly's dead."

"What!" Elizabeth's eyes widened in disbelief.

"I saw her. I had to leave or kill myself."

"Oh Uncle John . . ." Elizabeth said with sorrow in her voice. "She's alive and healthy and the baby too."

John stared at her—not daring to hope, wanting to believe. Tears welled in his eyes. He dropped his head into his hands and rocked and moaned.

Elizabeth hadn't seen him like this for years, and she didn't know if she could reach him. How he must have suffered believing Pearly was dead. Her heart hurt for him. She put her hand on his shoulder. "It's alright, Uncle John—it was just a mistake. Pearly loves you and wants you to come home—we all do."

It was as if she hadn't spoken.

Billy dropped the firewood he'd been carrying and peered over the edge.

"He thought your mom had died in childbirth," Elizabeth said quietly. "That's why he ran away."

Billy plopped down at the edge of the hole.

"Pa," he pleaded. "Come back to us."

The rocking stopped. Uncle John slowly raised his head and looked up at Billy.

"Let's go home. *Please!*" Tears were on Billy's cheeks.

Elizabeth looked from one to the other and felt a swell of joy. She wasn't the only one who cared desperately about Uncle John anymore. She wasn't the only one who could connect with him during his bad times. Relief washed over her. "Tell you what we're going to do now," she said. "Here's the plan . . ."

John and Elizabeth were now alone. Earlier Elizabeth and Billy had managed to get John out of the hole with his help and a lot of effort and pain. Then they had gone to work fashioning a makeshift stretcher out of a blanket and two saplings. One at each end, they had carried John back to the disappearing cabin, which did them the favor of being there.

Now Billy had gone back down the mountain to get help, and Elizabeth had stayed behind with Uncle John. "You sure you'll be alright?" she asked Billy anxiously. She'd proposed that she go and Billy stay with John but neither one of them would hear of it.

John laid a hand on her arm. "Let Billy go," he said quietly. "It'll work out for the best."

In the end, Elizabeth had sent Velvet with Billy. She held the little beagle's chin in her hand and looked into the brown eyes. "Home girl," she said. "Go home."

They settled into the cabin. There was a small store of canned goods and some packets of beef jerky. There was even an outhouse out back and also an old, rusty still, hidden behind some bushes. "Some moonshiners have been makin' illegal *hooch* up here," John said.

Elizabeth set about making them comfortable. She made up the wooden frame beds with their sleeping bags, then found an old broom and swept up a bit.

"All the luxuries," Uncle John smiled at her and eased himself carefully onto one of the beds.

She winced for him. "Does it hurt a lot?"

"Fair to middling," he said with a grin. "You still understand *mountainspeak*?"

"Shore enuff. So what do you want for lunch? How about beans straight out of the can," she laughed.

"Sounds good."

"How long do you think it will take him?" she asked lightly, scrounging for spoons in a drawer.

"Two days to home, I reckon." He didn't add what he was thinking—*if he doesn't have any trouble.* "Then he'll get some men together and come back after us." *What will we do if he doesn't make it, if he doesn't come back?* Elizabeth thought. She remembered the bear.

She brought a can of beans to him, spoon sticking from the open top, and sat on the bed with hers. She bowed her head and Uncle John did the same. "Thank you Father for this food and our many blessings," she began, eyes squeezed tight. "Please Lord, protect Billy and bring us help. In Jesus' name . . . Amen."

Chapter 12

Billy Alone

*G*OING DOWN THE *mountain is easier than coming up,* Billy thought, *and faster.* He'd made good time so far but still figured he had a couple of days before he would reach the farm.

Elizabeth had packed some food for him from the goods at the cabin but it wasn't enough for a growing boy's appetite, he reflected. He started dreaming of his mom's apple pie and fried chicken and biscuits soggy with butter.

"I'm hungry, aren't you girl?" he asked Velvet who was following at his heels. She wagged her tail happily—she knew they were going home.

He felt good, though. They'd found his step-dad and his leaving had all been a big mistake and not something Billy had done, as he had feared. He'd go get help and they'd carry John back down the mountain, Dr. Perkins would fix him up, and life would go on like before.

Except with a baby sister. "Emily, Emily Elizabeth." He tried the name out loud. He guessed it would be alright.

Billy remembered his *real* father because he was five when Zack died. Zack had taken him fishing sometimes on the weekends and played backyard catch with him. But he was always working in the mines trying to support his little family. Billy remembered him coming home "beat" from a shift underground and covered with soot. Before coming in for supper, he would bathe in the big zinc tub in the backyard. But still the coal dust was always with him—under his fingernails, in the creases around his eyes, in his lungs. Billy remembered the cough.

After the Pocahontas Mine disaster, his mom was sad a lot, crying at night when she didn't think he was awake. They'd moved back to her parents' house in Craigsville, and things slowly got better as Pearly got active at Alderson Baptist Church and went back to teaching. Then John McCreary was suddenly in their lives. When the couple married, they all moved to John's family's place.

These last five years, his mom had been very happy and so had Billy. He loved the freedom of the farm. John read with Billy and entertained the family around the fireplace at night with stories and Bible verses he'd memorized. He liked to draw and play the fiddle and had included Billy in these activities.

They also worked the farm together with family helping out. Elizabeth's cousin Clark was often over when he was needed, though he had a family of his own now. Pearly's brothers came and helped, too, when they could. John's dad had helped some when he was alive.

Billy's favorite time with John was when they worked with the farm animals. John had a special kinship with them and almost seemed able to read their minds. "See Bossy there," John would say pointing to one of the milk cows. "See how her ears are goin' back? Watch for that back right hoof. She's like to kick your milk bucket over." Billy had learned to appreciate each of the animals and its different personality. Even the pigs were all unique—like Rufus, who was very fastidious, ate politely, and was always grooming himself.

Billy was eager for things to get back to normal.

"I shore am hungry," he said again. The dog had forged ahead.

Then he saw the bee tree that John had raided. "Oh wow! Honeybees!" His mouth watered at the thought of honey. There were just a few bees going in and out of the hole in the tree, so he crept closer and climbed up on a low limb, crouching outside the entrance to the nest. If he just reached inside quickly and pulled out a hunk of honeycomb, it would last him for a while. He might get a couple of stings but the honey would taste sooo good.

He took a deep breath, stuck his hand inside the hole, and grabbed and sure enough, felt the comb and yanked off a piece. Immediately he jumped to the ground.

"Yum," he said aloud. Honey oozed from all the chambers of the honeycomb and dripped down his arm. He licked it off eagerly, savoring the sweet taste.

But suddenly behind him, he heard a loud buzzing; a swarm rose as one body and slammed down on him. They were all over him in an instant, stinging through clothes, thick on the exposed skin of his arms and face. Twenty stings. Thirty stings.

Billy dropped the comb and batted at the bees furiously, then ran through the woods hoping the branches would scrape some off. He grabbed a branch from the ground, scraping a bunch from his arm, tore off his jacket covered with bees and flung it into the bushes.

"Help me, Jesus," he cried.

But then ahead, he saw a stream with a pool in the middle and threw himself into it desperately, submerging totally in the deep part, picking persistent bees off underwater. He came up for air and went back under. Bees were flying around overhead. The next time he came up, they were mostly gone.

After a while, he dragged himself out of the water, groaning, and lay on the bank, picking the last straggler off his ankle. It felt like his body was on fire; the pain was everywhere. He knew of people that had died from as many bee stings as he'd gotten. He tried to calm down and think rationally.

Mud! he thought. Mud as it dried, sucked some of the poison out. As quickly as he was able, he peeled off the rest of his clothes and grabbed fistfuls of mud from the stream bank, slathering it on his face and arms and covering as much of his body as he could.

Then he lay back onto the grass and passed out.

Chapter 13

Waiting

IT HAD BEEN three days and nights. John and Elizabeth had talked about everything—talked more than they ever had.

Elizabeth would say, "Remember when I found Velvet in Charlie's hardware store in a box of puppies? We were all trapped by the rain and Grandpa wouldn't let me keep her but Mama insisted. Then he wouldn't let her in the car so you took her in your arms and carried her all the way home in the downpour."

She stopped to take a breath. "I thought you were so brave to stand up to Grandpa. You were my hero."

Uncle John smiled. "You wanted that pup so badly I thought you were gonna cry. I couldn't abide that."

And John would say, "You remember when your grandma Rose was dying? Them from the church was there and she wanted me to fiddle for her one last time, and she was my ma but I couldn't come out of my room because of all the people but *you* insisted?" He shook his head remembering. "You were so brave to come and get me like that . . . I only woulda come for you. You were *my* hero."

"Heroine," Elizabeth laughed but her eyes shone in the firelight. "Of course I remember—everyone was scared of you then."

"Remember that Christmas service at the church when you fiddled and Pearly sang? It was magical," Elizabeth sighed.

Uncle John gazed off into the distance. "When I thought she was dead, life was over for me," he said solemnly, with a catch in his voice.

"Well, she's not!" Elizabeth said. "And you have a baby daughter now! Emily Elizabeth!"

"Great name!" He grinned at her.

Elizabeth thought that he looked flushed. "Now, I'm just going to feel your forehead," she said, reaching out tentatively. In the past, Uncle John didn't like to be touched by anyone, but now he sat quietly as she put her hand to his head.

"I'm fine and dandy, Nurse Lizzie."

"How's your leg?"

"It's okay."

"Can I see it? Is it swollen or hot?"

"It's fine."

"Uncle John," she pleaded.

"What's for supper?" he said, to change the subject.

Elizabeth sighed, then gave up. "I thought I might try and get us a squirrel."

"With your slingshot? Lemme see it."

Elizabeth pulled it out of her back pocket and handed it over. John turned it over in his hand. "What kind of wood is the handle," he asked, examining the forked branch.

"I used mountain ash this time."

"Purty nice." He stretched it to try it out, sighting down the bands.

"I'll be back soon." Elizabeth said, taking it back and throwing a log on the campfire.

"Don't fall off the mountain," John said with a smile.

"Right."

Elizabeth went out to the rocky edge of the mountain and looked out over the hills and valleys. Surely Billy would be coming soon. No movement anywhere except for a small herd of deer crossing a clearing and a hawk floating on the air currents below. *Stop worrying! Help will come.*

She began searching for the right-sized rocks. She had been practicing with her slingshot almost every day after high school. Her family lived on a small farm outside of Fairmont now, where her father taught in college, her mom was a social worker, and she and her sisters went to school. When she got off the bus in the late afternoon, she changed clothes, fed and exercised her horse, and practiced with her slingshot.

She had never shot at an animal before the last week, though—at trees, at empty soup cans, but never at something alive. She knew, though, that some hunters used slingshots for small game and that they could be quite deadly.

She loved all animals—livestock, pets, wildlife—but she was a farm girl at heart; she had seen pigs butchered for meat for the winter and the heads of chickens chopped off to make Sunday dinner. Uncle John was hungry, and they had to eat.

It only took a half hour of silent watching until two squirrels appeared, frisking in the branches overhead, chasing each other in a spiral down the tree trunks, sprinting between the trees. Without a moment's hesitation, Elizabeth loaded a stone in the pouch and pulled back the bands, sighting along their length. Meat for supper.

Chapter 14

Moonshiners

SOMETHING WAS LICKING his face. Billy opened one swollen eyelid and stared straight into Velvet's chocolate eyes. The pup wagged her tail happily. He sat up and then regretted it as the woods whirled around him. He lay back down carefully and Velvet resumed her licking. "It's okay, girl. I'm alive—I'll get up."

Billy rolled onto his hands and knees, still dizzy. His arms and legs were painful and swollen from the poison of the stings, and when he crawled to the edge of the stream to look at himself in the water, his puffy face frightened him.

He slid into the water, its coolness easing some of the pain. Soon he was feeling better and sloshed around, washing off the mud pack and ducking under the surface. He fetched his clothes, picking the dead bees off them, washed them out, and spread them on the bank in the sun to dry. Then he crawled into the shade and lay down, exhausted from his efforts.

How long was I out? he wondered. No way to tell—he peered up at the sun's position. He had to get help for John and Elizabeth, but he was *so* tired.

The next time he woke up it was late in the day, and shadows were long. He groaned and sat up groggily. Velvet was sleeping on his clothes where he had left them. He felt better but hungry now. He pulled some jerky out of the pocket of his pants and chewed on it. Velvet's nose twitched, and she came to sit beside him—hopeful. He broke off a piece and gave her some, got a drink of water, and put on his dry clothes.

"Ready to try again?" he said to the little dog. She panted eagerly and trotted behind him out of the clearing.

After they had eaten, Elizabeth took the leftovers out into the woods to dump them. It wouldn't do to attract hungry animals in the night.

As she came back toward the cabin, she heard voices and ducked behind some bushes, peering over carefully. John was propped up against a tree stump with his hurt leg stretched out. Two men were standing over him. They were scruffy-looking—old felt hats on their heads, worn clothes, scuffed boots.

"I'm agonna ask you one more time," the tall one said. "What be ye doin' here?"

Uncle John was silent. Elizabeth could see that he'd gone *into* himself. He had that withdrawn, shut down look to his face.

The tall man grabbed John's arm and he flinched.

"Let him alone!" Elizabeth stepped into the clearing.

"Whoa . . . what do we have here, Milton? The mute's got a girl and a purty one at that."

"I'm his niece. Leave him be."

"His *niece,* you say." The tall man laughed and Milton joined in, showing a mouthful of crooked, rotting teeth. "You know what I think, Milton? I think these two are up here spying on our *operation,*" he said, obviously proud of the word. He drew a knife out of his boot. "And we don't like spies. Planning to report us to the revenuers and collect a little reward maybe?"

"We're not spies," Elizabeth said carefully, "and we don't care about your still or your moonshine."

The man's eyes narrowed. "Then what are you doing way up here? Out for a Sunday walk?" he sneered.

"We just . . ." How could she explain?

"And what's wrong with thisn' here?" The man nudged Uncle John with the toe of his grimy boot.

Suddenly, Uncle John came to life, yanked the moonshiner's leg out from under him, and he fell, dropping the knife.

Milton was shocked into immobility for a second. Without a thought, Elizabeth pulled the slingshot from her pocket, loaded a rock, and got him in the back of the head. He sank to the ground.

John's and Elizabeth's eyes met across the clearing.

The tall man groaned and sat up, rubbing his head. He looked at Milton lying on the ground and at Elizabeth with her slingshot reloaded and aimed at his forehead.

Uncle John had his rifle out now and cocked it. "Git your friend and your equipment and skedaddle," he said.

"You come back, we won't be near so neighborly," Elizabeth added.

Chapter 15

Pearly Blue

JOHN AND ELIZABETH weren't the only ones waiting. Pearly sat in the rocking chair by the potbelly stove nursing her baby daughter. She didn't know what time it was but she hadn't heard the rooster yet. The stove had been bedded down for the night but the embers still glowed so there was some warmth.

Soft brown curls falling around her face swayed as she rocked to and fro, to and fro. Emily nursed contentedly but then flinched when a tear fell on her pink forehead. Pearly wiped the baby's face with a clean cloth diaper and then blotted her own eyes.

"Poor baby," she said, kissing one plump cheek, "your daddy's run off."

Why did he leave? Was the care of a child too much for him? Was he scared? Doesn't he love me anymore? She had asked herself a hundred questions since he left. She understood John's fears only too well, but this didn't make sense to her. All she knew was that he took all her hopes and dreams with him up the mountain. Had she been wrong to allow Billy to follow Elizabeth? "Please Lord," she whispered, "protect them all and bring John back to me."

She remembered the first time she'd ever spoken to John. And she remembered the dance.

Pearly Blue was in her last year of high school; John no longer went to school because of the bullying. It was the early twentieth century, and schools were in no way set up to handle "problem" students. Miss Carpenter hadn't forgotten John, though. She often sent home books with his brothers and sisters. He devoured and usually memorized them. She even visited the farm occasionally to see if he understood the math problems.

Pearly remembered John as a boy, remembered his photographic memory and remembered the problems with bullies who were jealous of his abilities. *Freak,* they called him. The girls were drawn to him, though, drawn by the blue eyes, the curly, dark hair—the mix of intelligence, mystery, and danger.

But once he no longer attended school, he was mostly forgotten, but not by Pearly. She still saw John at church functions and occasionally in town when he came with his dad for supplies.

Over the years, he had grown into a handsome young man, and Pearly became a beauty with a sweet personality to match. Pearly admired his talents and had seen some of his art decorating the church classrooms. She had heard him fiddle at several dances with his brothers on banjo and guitar.

John had been watching Pearly, too. *You don't have a chance with her,* he told himself repeatedly.

One beautiful October day, Pearly went for a walk with her cousin Eliza. The girls brought books along and their embroidery and ended up at Barth's Pond near the dirt road into Craigsville. They sat on a log by the water and gossiped about the dance coming up in mid-November at the community center.

"I'm going to wear my aunt's blue dress with the little flowers on it," Pearly said.

"My mom's making me a new one, and it's going to be pale pink," Eliza said excitedly.

"I love to dance," Pearly sighed.

"Ain't you worried about what Reverend Brown will say?" Eliza asked. The Baptist church was against dancing.

Pearly picked at an embroidery thread on her sewing. "He won't be there. Besides, David dances in the Bible."

Just then John came over the hill, driving the family's flatbed wagon drawn by a bay horse.

"Look! It's John McCreary!" Eliza exclaimed. "We'd better git home; my ma says not to speak to him because he's dangerous."

"I think he's nice," Pearly said, eyes fixed on John, who, not seeing the girls under the trees, had turned the horse aside for a drink of water at the pond.

"He coming this way," Eliza said in a frightened whisper. "I'm going home. Ain't you comin'?"

"No, I think I'll stay a bit," Pearly said calmly, directing her attention to her sewing.

"You're gonna get in trouble," Eliza hurried toward their farmhouse in the distance.

John jumped from the wagon and led the horse to the water, watching it drink, reins held loosely in one hand. Sensing something, he looked up and caught sight of Pearly on the log.

She smiled, "Hi."

He dropped his eyes to the water.

She got off the log and walked towards him. "What's your horse's name?"

John hesitated. "Mike," he said finally.

"He's a beauty." Pearly stroked the shiny brown neck.

John's eyes rested on the girl. *The horse isn't the only one who's a beauty,* he thought.

There was brief silence. They watched as a large fish came close to the shore and looked at them through the water then flipped his tail and swam away.

"I got the best new book for my birthday," Pearly said, drawing it from her bag and showing him the front cover.

John took it from her.

"Would you like to borrow it?"

"Ain't you reading it?"

"I've just finished."

He held the book tentatively by one corner.

"Are you playing at the dance at the center next month?" Pearly asked, her heart pounding.

"I reckon."

"I'll be there. You could return it then."

"Mighty nice of you." A bit of a smile flitted across his face.

"You deserve for people to be nice to you," she said earnestly.

But just then . . . shouts in the distance from the farmhouse. "Pearly! Pearleeee! You come on home now y'hear!"

John started and pulled the horse's muzzle up out of the water. "You'd best go," he said.

Pearly sighed and picked up her shawl from the log. "Let me know what you think of the book," she said over her shoulder.

Chapter 16

The Dance

A WEEK BEFORE THE dance, Pearly's mother was working on the dress. This involved Pearly standing on a stool while her mom pinned up the hem and took in the waist a bit. Pearly was troubled and in a fog. Zack had asked her to the dance and after her family's encouragement, she had said yes. But all along she had planned to just go with her family and see John, maybe dance with him.

"Pearly Blue, I asked you twice to turn to the side," her mom looked up at her in exasperation. She had straight pins clamped in the corner of her mouth and more pinned to the front of her apron.

Pearly turned obediently a quarter turn. "Sorry Mama. Thanks for fixing the dress."

The evening of the dance, the dress fit perfectly, comfortable against her small waist, grazing the top of her ankles. It was the 1920s, but back in the hills no one was wearing short skirts or bobbing their hair. In fact, Reverend Brown preached against that very thing one recent Sunday.

The Craigsville Community Center was gaily decorated. The Women's Club had been there in the morning to hang crepe paper and direct the men to arrange tables and chairs. Colored tablecloths covered the dessert tables, and the punch bowl had a table all its own. Families were in attendance as well as couples and singles. There were line dances and circle dances where you didn't need a partner, an occasional waltz, and even music you could clog to. Bertram Higgenbotham was the best clogger and put on quite a show with the teen boys trying to keep up. Banjos and fiddles were everywhere but there were also harmonicas and jugs and a stray washboard. Loosely formed groups took turns playing; one man was twanging a jaw harp. It was an *event*!

But the weather had turned, to everyone's dismay, and there was a freak early snowstorm brewing. Most people planned to leave early if it began to snow.

John McCreary and his brothers Jim and Dan weren't slated to play until later in the evening so they arrived a bit late when the party was in full swing.

John had been looking forward to this all month because of his chance meeting with Pearly, and tonight he looked his best in a red flannel shirt and clean coveralls. He had her book inside his fiddle case and planned to return it and maybe discuss it over punch. Not many of the community took the time to treat him kindly and talk to him like she had. Maybe he'd even dance with her. He felt a blush warm his cheeks at the thought. Maybe he'd even ask her to marry him. He knew that was crazy, and his imagination was on fire, but there it was.

He entered the hall, scanning for Pearly, then caught sight of her in a knot of people at the refreshment table. She glowed in a blue dress, her hair down on her shoulders and shining. He started towards her just as she saw him and smiled, but then Zack stepped between them.

"C'mon Pearly, let's dance," he said, guiding her onto the dance floor.

John understood immediately. She was with Zack. He had misunderstood her kindness . . . it had been pity. He could feel his face getting hot, hear a rushing in his ears. He turned to the nearest table and with one stroke of his arm, swept cakes and pies onto the floor with a crash.

Music stopped, everyone stared open-mouthed.

Pearly's eyes filled with tears, and Zack put an arm around her.

John yanked open the door and ran out into the cold, leaving his coat, the book, and his fiddle. He walked four miles home, oblivious to everything as the snow began to fall and turned into a howling blizzard. The next day he was sick, and later that week was diagnosed with pneumonia and put in the hospital in Summersville, where he remained for six weeks.

He was never the same. The physical and emotional trauma of the evening exacerbated his symptoms to the point that he was now withdrawn, brooding. The family tired of trying to relate to him. The community shunned him.

Pearly went on to marry Zack.

Chapter 17

Rescue

THEIR FOOD WAS running low. Elizabeth foraged as best she could—picked berries, brought down small game with her slingshot. John had gotten quieter, and that worried her. She believed he was feeling more pain now; his cheeks were flushed. She pushed the bushes aside and looked where she had seen a rabbit's nest yesterday but it was empty. She trudged on.

Where is Billy? She sighed.

Maybe she'd been wrong to trust a ten-year-old boy. Maybe she should have gone herself. Something could have happened to him. He could have gotten hurt in any number of ways, could have gotten lost. She felt tension in her neck and shoulders. Mustn't get discouraged. *Lord, give me strength.*

There was just no game today. It was gray and sprinkling and animals were in hiding. She hated to go back empty handed with her stomach growling. What would they eat tonight?

She turned and went back by way of the raspberry bushes, picking and dropping them with muffled *plunks* in a little pot she had brought along.

"Raspberries again," she said cheerfully, holding them up as she entered the camp.

John was before the fire, stirring it with a stick. He didn't look up. She sat across from him and began picking through the berries, removing stems and leaves and dividing them into two bowls. She passed him a bowl, and he took it silently. "You got a boyfriend?" he said suddenly.

"No one steady," Elizabeth said with a smile. "I'll be going off to college this fall though; maybe I'll meet someone there."

"You still got a heap of living to do," he said. "I think you should try walking out. Leave me here."

"Never!" She was shocked.

"I want you to go. I don't need no company." He stood unsteadily, leaning on the walking stick, and she rose also. "I said *git!*"

She knew what he was trying to do, but still it stung. "I'm not leaving you. Nothing you say can make me."

He took a step toward her, then stopped. It was a standoff. "Please go," he said softly. "Save yourself."

Then they heard it—shouts down the mountainside.

Elizabeth ran to the edge of the clearing. She could see men moving below. "Haallooo," one of them called out. She saw Billy's blond hair flash through the leaves. "Billy! Up here!" she yelled, jumping up and down and waving her arms.

That night they sat around the fire halfway down the mountain. The five men that had come with Billy smoked and drank coffee. Elizabeth's cousin Clark was among them. "Are you alright?" he said. "Your mom and dad are totally hysterical."

"I'm fine," she grinned. "Just hungry." She took the chicken wing out of his hand and took a bite.

Clark laughed. "You always were a brat."

The doctor had come with the young men, although he was huffing and puffing by the time they had reached the cabin. He'd brought along a stretcher and his bag and stabilized Uncle John's leg, giving him penicillin and aspirin.

Then four people at a time carried him through the woods until nightfall, switching off when they grew tired. Elizabeth and Billy both insisted on a turn. Elizabeth worried that the jouncing going downhill must hurt John but he didn't make a sound.

By late afternoon of the next day, the farmhouse was in sight, which lifted everyone's spirits except for John's. He feared facing Pearly.

Dark thoughts roamed through his mind like wild animals. Pearly must be furious that he left. Perhaps she didn't want to be with him anymore. Maybe she hated him. She might take Billy and the baby and move out, back in with her parents. He prayed silently that she would forgive him.

Velvet took off at a full run for home, bounding over the grasses. Billy ran after her, free to be a kid again.

And then there was someone else running in the field—Pearly Blue, hampered by the weeds and her skirt.

Elizabeth saw John's face contort as he lay on the stretcher and knew it wasn't the bumps and jolts because they were in the smooth upper meadow. She reached down and took his hand.

"It'll be alright."

"Put me down," John called out to the stretcher-bearers, sitting up. The men obeyed and he rose shakily, leaning on the walking stick. He'd at least face Pearly standing on his own two feet. When she was ten feet away, he began the speech he had prepared in his head. "Pearly . . ."

But before he could get any further, she was in his arms. He breathed deeply of the sweet smell of her hair, dared to hold her close. She pulled back a bit and looked into his eyes.

The others moved away self-consciously.

He started again, "Pearly . . ."

"Shhhhh . . ." She stopped his lips with her fingers. "You're back and that's all that matters," she said kissing him gently. "Let's go home. Your daughter is anxious to meet you."

Elizabeth, watching them, smiled through tears of joy.

As the men helped John back onto the stretcher, Pearly turned to Elizabeth, tears sparkling in her eyes too.

"Thank you for bringing him back to me," she said softly.

John, from his position on the stretcher, nodded up at her. "You brought us together, and you brought us back together."

Elizabeth smiled at them both and then, releasing him to Pearly, took off at a jog through the meadow.

"Billy! Wait for me!" she shouted, her heart light.

All was right with the world.

Epilogue

PEARLY AND JOHN were waiting by the gate for Elizabeth's departure. Her car was packed and sitting at a slant on the hill, emergency brake in position.

"But Pearly," John was saying. "I thought you were dead!"

"Even if I did die, you can't run away because of Billy and Emily Elizabeth. Promise you won't run away again."

"I promise," Uncle John looked at her steadily.

"No matter what," Pearly added.

Uncle John took both of her hands in his, like he had at their wedding. "No matter what," he said.

Elizabeth watched them through the screen and then stepped out into the morning sunshine, backpack over one shoulder. She looked up Tyler's Mountain with feelings of both nostalgia and triumph, then went to join the two.

"Here she is," said Pearly.

Billy came around from the backyard.

"You keep saving my life," said John, looking at her. Then he smiled, "You're like a superhero!"

Elizabeth laughed. "Wonder Woman! You are *so* worth saving," she added seriously.

"This time you saved the whole family."

Elizabeth blushed.

"You're the one who's special now," he added.

They looked at each other, then both looked away.

"I gotta go," she said.

"You coming for Thanksgiving?" John followed her out to her car, limping slightly.

"You betcha. Maybe Mama and Daddy and my sisters will come. They'll want to see the baby."

"I'll let Emily know to expect you."

"Maybe she'll have *the gift*—that intuition thing," Elizabeth mused.

"Mebbe so."

John leaned on the top of the gate and watched her roll down the hill, wave out the window and drive toward the hard road. Pearly had Emily now, waving the baby's hand. Billy stood watching her departure with both hands shoved in his pockets, like he didn't care.

"There she goes back to her life," Pearly said.

Epilogue

John was silent, putting his arm around her shoulders and offering a finger for Emily to hold. They all gazed at a cloud drifting lazily across the blue sky, at grasses swaying in the fields, brightly colored flower heads bobbing. There were the sounds of the farm—insects buzzing, roosters crowing, a horse whinnying somewhere up near the barn.

And the mountains, always the mountains. The life they held so dear.

"We are blessed," Pearly said.

"Shore enuff," John agreed.

Contact Information

To order additional copies of this book, please visit
www.redemption-press.com.
Also available on Amazon.com and BarnesandNoble.com
Or by calling toll free 1-844-2REDEEM.